HELLO KI

presents the **S**torybook Collection

The Little
Mermaid

Abrams Books for Young Readers
New York

In the deep, blue sea lived a mermaid named Hello Kitty.
She was known throughout the realm for her beautiful singing
voice. She loved her home, but she longed to see life on land.

She had heard stories of the villages on land and was curious about the people who lived there. She imagined what flowers smelled like and how it sounded when birds sang.

Most of all, she wanted to feel the sun.
Sadly, Hello Kitty had to wait until she was a little older
before she could swim to the surface of the sea.

Years passed, until finally Hello Kitty was old enough to swim to the surface. The sky was radiant, and the waves glistened like jewels.

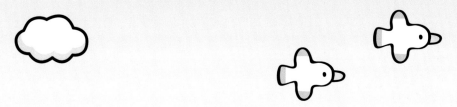

She swam close to the shore, where pink sea roses grew.
She could smell their sweet scent even from the water.

When evening came, Hello Kitty pulled herself onto a rock so she could see all around her. Off in the distance, she heard music and saw a ship covered in lights. It was a birthday celebration for a prince!

The lights and music were so beautiful, and the prince was so handsome, that Hello Kitty did not notice the dark clouds gathering.

Soon, hard rains fell and strong winds blew.
The wind whipped the waves around the prince's boat. The boat
rocked so hard, the prince was thrown overboard.

Hello Kitty dove until she found the prince. With the help of her dolphin friend, she carried him back to the shore.

Hello Kitty could not stop thinking about the prince.
She spent her days and nights singing sad, beautiful songs.

Finally, Hello Kitty asked the Sea Witch for help. The Sea Witch offered Hello Kitty a potion, but it came with a warning.

If Hello Kitty drank the potion, it would turn her mermaid tail into legs. She'd be able to walk on land and be with the prince. But she would also lose her voice. If the prince didn't fall in love with her, Hello Kitty would lose her voice forever.

Hello Kitty thought long and hard. If she couldn't talk,
how could she get to know the prince? But if she couldn't
walk, she might never see the prince again!

Hello Kitty decided to take a chance. She swam
to the surface and drank the potion.
She felt her mermaid tail change into two legs.

She walked out of the water and across the sand to the prince's castle.

The prince was hosting a ball that night. Hello Kitty arrived just in time to dance with the prince. As they danced, the prince asked Hello Kitty her name. She could not answer.

Suddenly, the prince recognized Hello Kitty!
She was the one who had rescued him when he
fell into the sea!

To show his gratitude, the prince kissed Hello Kitty's cheek. Hello Kitty's voice returned! She sang the prince and his guests the most beautiful song and everyone was very happy.

The Library of Congress has catalogued the hardcover edition of this book as follows:

Hello Kitty the little mermaid / by Sanrio Co., Ltd.
pages cm. — (Hello Kitty storybook)
ISBN 978-1-4197-1825-0 (hardcover) — ISBN 978-1-61312-859-6 (ebook)
I. Andersen, H. C. (Hans Christian), 1805–1875. Lille havfrue. English. II. Sanrio, Kabushiki Kaisha. III. Title:
The little mermaid.
PZ8.H3696 2016
[E]—dc23
2015015277

ISBN for this edition: 978-1-4197-2549-4

Printed and bound in China
10 9 8 7 6 5 4 3 2 1

For bulk discount inquiries,
contact specialsales@abramsbooks.com
or the address below.

ABRAMS The Art of Books
115 West 18th Street, New York, NY 10011
abramsbooks.com